The Princess and the Lion and other princess stories

Compiled by Tig Thomas

Miles Kelly

First published in 2013 by Miles Kelly Publishing Ltd
Harding's Barn, Bardfield End Green, Thaxted, Essex, CM6 3PX, UK

2 4 6 8 10 9 7 5 3 1

Publishing Director Belinda Gallagher
Creative Director Jo Cowan
Editorial Director Rosie McGuire
Senior Editor Claire Philip
Senior Designer Joe Jones
Production Manager Elizabeth Collins
Reprographics Stephan Davis, Jennifer Hunt, Thom Allaway

ISBN 978-1-78209-219-3

Printed in China

British Library Cataloguing-in-Publication Data
A catalogue record for this book is available from the British Library

ACKNOWLEDGEMENTS

The publishers would like to thank the following artists who have contributed to this book:
Marcin Piwowarski, Mélanie Florian (inc. cover), Jennie Poh

All other artwork from the Miles Kelly Artwork Bank

The publishers would like to thank the following sources for the use of their photographs:
Cover frame: Karina Bakalyan/Shutterstock.com
Inside frame: asmjp/Shutterstock.com

Made with paper from a sustainable forest

www.mileskelly.net info@mileskelly.net

Contents

The Riddle

By the Brothers Grimm

A HANDSOME PRINCE ONCE HAD a great desire to travel the world, so he set off, taking no one with him but a trusty servant. One day he came to a great forest. Evening drew on but he couldn't find shelter and he could not find anywhere to spend the night. All of a sudden he came across a little crooked house.

The prince guessed that he had come to a witch's house, but as by this time it was quite dark and he could go no further, he knocked on the door, and stepped inside.

An old woman sat in an armchair near

the fire, and as the prince and his servant entered she turned her red eyes to them. Her daughter stood in the corner of the room, and looked at them nervously.

"Good evening," muttered the old woman, "Won't you sit down?"

As she stoked the fire on which she was cooking something in a little pot, her daughter came forward and secretly warned the travellers to be very careful and not to eat or drink anything, as the old woman's brews were dangerous.

They went to bed and slept soundly until the morning. When they were ready to set off, and the prince had mounted his horse, the old woman said, "Wait a minute, I must give you a drink." Whilst she went to fetch it the prince rode off, and the servant who had waited to tighten his saddle was alone when she returned.

"Take this to your master," she said, but as she spoke the glass cracked and poison spurted over the horse. It was so powerful that the poor creature fell down dead.

The servant ran after his master and told him what had happened, then, not wishing to lose the saddle as well as the horse, he went back to fetch it. When he got to the spot he saw that a raven had perched on the poor horse and was pecking at it. "Who knows whether we shall get anything better to eat today!" said the servant, and he shot the raven and carried it off.

At nightfall the prince and his servant reached an inn. The servant gave the landlord the raven to cook for their supper. As it happened, the inn was a meeting place for a band of villains.

As soon as it was dark, the twelve villains arrived, with the intention of killing and robbing the strangers. Before they set to work, however, they sat down at the table, and greedily ate the raven broth meant for the prince and his servant. They had only taken a couple of spoonfuls when they all fell down dead, for the poison had passed from the horse to the raven and into the broth. The prince and his servant left the inn without any dinner, and rode on.

After travelling all night they reached a town where there lived a lovely but most arrogant princess. She had issued a proclamation that any man who asked her a riddle that she herself was unable to answer could marry her, but should she guess the riddle he must lose his head.

She claimed three days in which to think over the riddles, but she was so very clever that she always guessed them in a much shorter time. Nine suitors had already lost their lives when the prince arrived, but dazzled by her beauty, he was determined to risk his life in hope of winning her.

So he came before her and told his riddle. “What is this?” he asked. “One slew none and yet killed twelve.”

The princess could not think what it was! She thought and thought, and looked through all her books of riddles and puzzles, but she found nothing to help her, and could not guess. In fact, she was at her wits’ end. As she could think of no way to guess the riddle, she ordered her maid to sneak into the prince's bedroom at night and listen in case he talked in his dreams, betraying the secret. But the clever servant had taken his master's place, and when the maid came into the room he tore off the cloak she had wrapped herself in and shooed her off.

On the second night the princess sent her lady-in-waiting, hoping that she might succeed better. But this time the servant took away her mantle and chased her away.

On the third night the prince thought he would be safe, so he went to bed. But in the middle of the night the princess herself came, all huddled up in a cloak, and sat down near him. When she thought he was fast asleep, she spoke to him, hoping he would answer in the middle of his dreams, as many people do.

But he was wide awake all the time, and

heard and understood everything she said.

Then she asked, "One slew none. What does that mean?"

And he answered, "A raven, which fed on the body of a poisoned horse."

She went on, "And yet killed twelve – what is that?"

"Those are twelve villains who ate the raven and died of it," he said.

As soon as she knew the riddle she tried to slip away, but he held onto her cloak so tightly that she was obliged to leave it.

The next morning the princess announced that she had guessed the riddle, and sent for the twelve judges, before whom she gave her answer. But the prince begged to be heard too, and said, "She came last night to question me, otherwise she never could have guessed the meaning of the riddle."

The servant brought out the three cloaks, and when the judges saw the grey one they said to her, "Let it be embroidered with gold for it shall be your wedding cloak."

The Three Captured Princesses

By Andrew Lang

THERE WAS ONCE a king and a queen who had three wonderfully beautiful daughters, and their one thought, from morning till night, was how they could make the girls happy.

One day the princesses said to the king, "Dear father, we would like to have a picnic in the country."

And so the royal family stepped into a

carriage and drove away into the country. The drive had made them hungry, and they ate until almost all of the food had gone.

When the princesses had finished eating, they said to their parents, "Now we should like to wander about the woods a little, but when you want to go home, just call to us." And they ran off.

Meanwhile the king and queen sat lazily

among the heather. The sun was dropping towards the horizon, and after a while they began to think it was time to go home. They called to their daughters but no one answered them.

Frightened at the silence, they searched the wood, but no trace of the girls was to be found anywhere. The earth seemed to have swallowed them up. The queen wept all the way home, and the king issued a proclamation saying that whoever should bring back his lost daughters would have one of them to marry.

Living in the palace was a faithful servant of the king's called Bensurdatu, and when he saw how sad the king was he said to him, "Your majesty, let me go and seek your daughters."

"No, no, Bensurdatu," replied the king.

"Three daughters have I lost, and I shall not lose you also."

But Bensurdatu said again, "Let me go, and I will bring back your daughters."

The king gave in, and Bensurdatu set out. He rode for many miles, and at length he saw a light in the window of a tiny hut.

"Who goes there?" asked a voice, as he knocked at the door.

"Please can you give me a night's shelter," replied Bensurdatu, "I am a traveller and I have lost my way."

The door was opened by a very old woman who asked what his business was.

"Ah, good woman, I have a hard task," answered Bensurdatu, "I have to find the king's daughters and bring them home!"

"Oh, unhappy man," cried she, "you know not what you are doing!"

"Oh, tell me, if you know where they are, my good woman," he begged, "for with them lies all our happiness."

"Even if I were to tell you," answered she, "you could not rescue them. To do that you would have to go to the bottom of a deep river, and there they are guarded by ogres."

Bensurdatu thanked the woman and said he was going to try his luck. The sun had only just risen above the hills next morning when Bensurdatu woke and set off for the river. But he did not leave before borrowing the old woman's bucket and chain from her well. When he came to the banks of the river he cut two sturdy poles and set up the bucket and chain over them, then let himself down into the river.

Terrible thunder and noise rose up around him but he thought to himself, 'Oh, make as

much noise
as you like, it
won't hurt me!'

He wandered for a time, then found himself in a large, brilliantly lit hall, and in the middle sat the eldest princess. In front of her lay a huge, fearsome ogre, fast asleep. The princess saw Bensurdatu, nodded to him, and asked with her eyes how he had come to be there.

For an answer he drew his sword, and cut off the ogre's head with such a blow that it flew into the corner. The heart of the princess leapt within her, and she placed a golden crown on the head of Bensurdatu, and called him her rescuer.

"Now show me where your sisters are," he said. So the princess opened a door, and led him into another hall, and in there sat one of her sisters, guarded by a second sleeping ogre. When the second princess saw them, she made a sign to them to hide themselves, for the ogre was waking up.

"I smell man's flesh!" it murmured.

"How could any man get down here?" asked the princess. "Go to sleep again." And as soon as the ogre closed its eyes, Bensurdatu ran out from his corner, and struck such a blow that the ogre's head flew far, far away. The princess placed her golden crown in Bensurdatu's hand.

"Now show me where your youngest sister is," said he, "so that I can free her."

"Ah! That I fear you will never be able to do," they sighed, "for she is in the power of a serpent with seven heads."

"Take me to it," replied Bensurdatu. "It will be a splendid fight."

Then the princess opened a door, and Bensurdatu passed through. He found himself in a hall that was even larger than the other two.

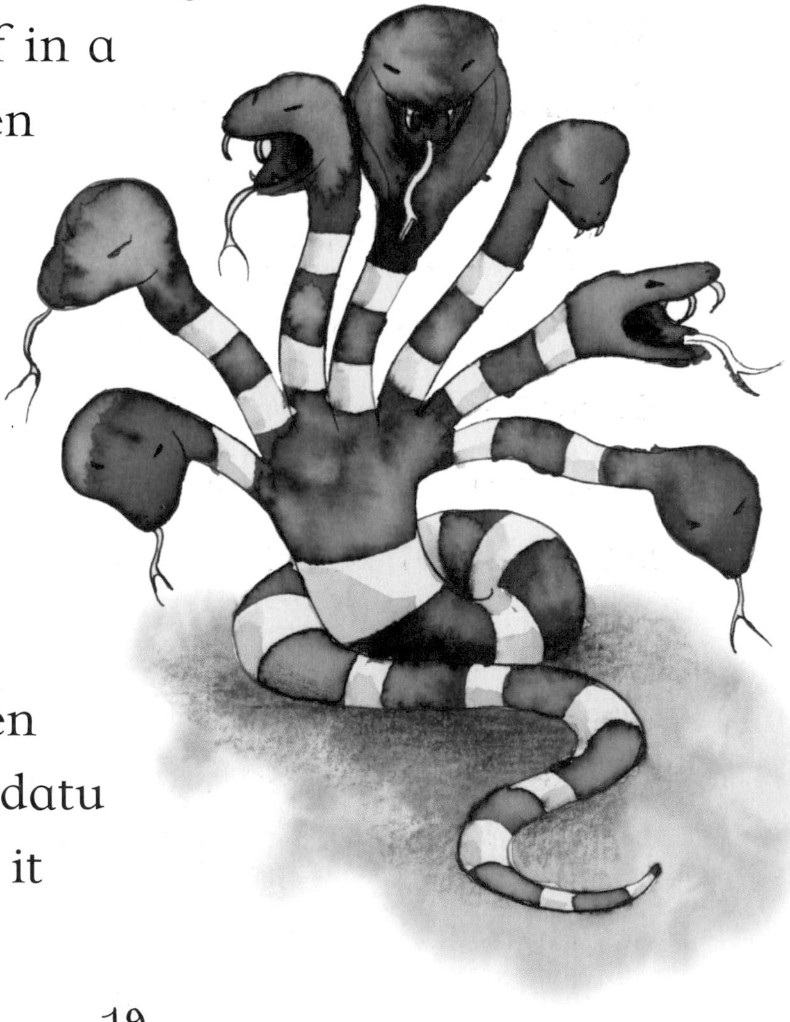

There stood the youngest sister, chained to the wall, and before her was a serpent with seven heads. As Bensurdatu stepped forwards it twisted its seven heads in his direction, and then made a quick dart to snatch him.

But Bensurdatu drew his sword and swung it about, until each of the seven heads were rolling on the floor. Flinging down his sword he rushed to the princess and broke her chains. She took off her golden crown and placed it in his hand.

The king and queen were full of joy when they saw their daughters once more. They all sat down to a feast, and there were great rejoicings. A wedding was ordered, and celebrations were held for three days for the marriage of Bensurdatu and the youngest princess – and they lived happily ever after.

The Princess and the Lion

A traditional Spanish fairy tale

THERE WAS ONCE a very pretty girl who worked as a cowherd. One morning, when she was driving her cows through the meadows she heard a loud groan. She rushed to the spot and found that the noise came from a lion, which lay stretched upon the ground.

You can guess how frightened she was! But the lion seemed in so much pain that she drew nearer until she saw he had a large thorn in one foot. She pulled out the thorn, bound up the paw, and the lion was very grateful. He licked her hand with his big rough tongue.

When the girl had finished, she went back to find the cows, but they had gone, and though she hunted everywhere she could not find them. Her master scolded her bitterly for losing the cows.

After that she had to take the donkeys to the woods to feed, until one morning, she heard a groan, which sounded quite human. She went straight to the source of the noise, and saw the same lion lying with a deep wound across his face.

This time she was not afraid at all, and ran towards him, washing the wound and laying soothing herbs upon it. When she had bound it up the lion thanked her in the same manner as before.

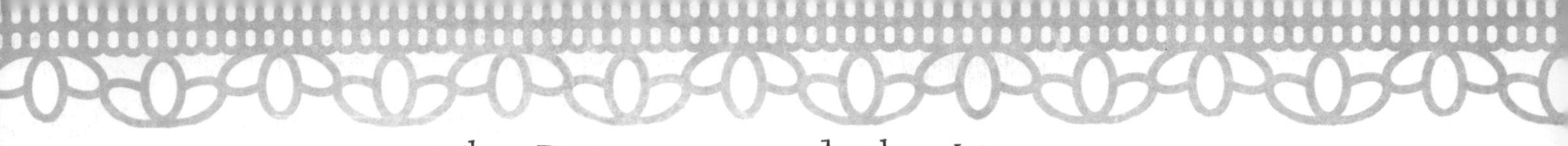

After that she returned to her herd of donkeys, but they were nowhere to be seen. She searched but they had vanished!

Then she had to go home and confess to her master, who scolded her severely. "Now go," he said, "and see to the pigs!"

So the next day she took the pigs out, and found them such good feeding grounds that they grew fatter every day.

A year passed by, and one morning when the maiden was out with her pigs she heard a groan. She ran to see what it was, and found her old friend the lion, wounded, lying under a tree. She washed his wounds one by one, and laid healing herbs upon them. And the lion licked her hands. After he had gone she ran to the place where she had left her pigs, but they had vanished.

The maiden looked everywhere and at

last she thought that if she climbed a tree she might see them. But as soon as she was up the tree, something happened that made her forget the pigs. A handsome young man was coming down the path, and when he had almost reached the tree he pulled aside a rock and disappeared behind it.

The maiden rubbed her eyes and waited, and at dawn the next morning the rock moved to one side and a lion came out. The maiden thought to herself, 'I will not move from here until I discover who that man is.'

That evening the young man came back, so she came down from the tree and begged him to tell her his name. The young man looked very pleased to see her, and said that he was a prince enchanted by a powerful giant, and all day he was forced to appear as the lion whom she had so often helped.

More than this, it was the giant who had stolen her animals as revenge.

So the girl asked what she could do to reverse the enchantment. He said the only way was weave a cloak using a lock of hair from the head of a princess.

"Very well," answered the girl, "I will go to the city, and knock at the door of the king's palace, and ask the princess to take me as a servant." She went straight to the palace to ask for work.

"You will have to do kitchen work," she was told, and she agreed.

Every day the maiden arranged her hair, and made herself look very neat and smart. Everyone admired and praised her, until the princess heard of it. She sent for the girl, and when she saw how nicely she had dressed her hair, the princess told her she was to come and comb hers.

Now the hair of the princess was very thick and long, and shone like the sun. The girl combed it until it was brighter than ever. The princess was pleased, and told her to come every day until the girl begged permission to cut off one lock.

The princess, who was very proud of her hair, did not like the idea of parting with any of it, but she said, “You may have it, then, on condition that you shall find me a handsome prince to marry!”

And the girl answered that she would try. She cut off the lock, and wove it into a coat that glittered like silk, and brought it to the young man. He told her to carry it straight to the giant. So the maiden climbed up the mountain, but before she reached the top the giant heard her, and rushed out breathing

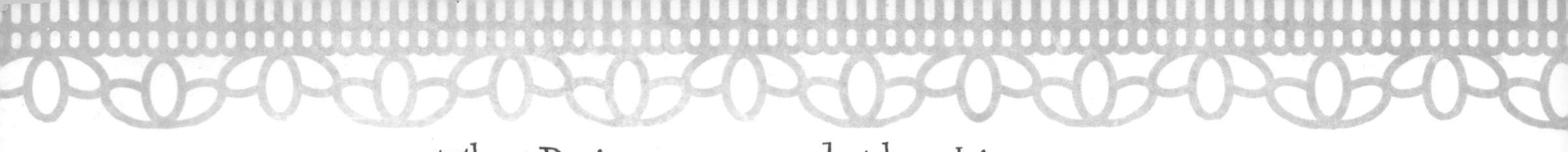

fire and flame. She called out that she had brought him the coat, and he grew quiet.

The giant tried on the coat, and was pleased. As a reward the maiden said that she wanted the giant to take the spell off the lion.

The giant would not hear of it at first, but in the end he gave in. He told her to lead the lion into a nearby stream. The prince would come out of the water, free from the enchantment.

So in the morning when the prince became a lion, she took him to the stream, and out of the water came the prince.

The young man thanked the maiden for all she had done for him, and asked if she would marry him. But the maiden answered sadly that she had promised the princess that the prince would marry her.

So they went to see the princess together – but when the princess saw the young man, a great joy filled her heart, for he was her brother, who had been enchanted and lost.

He told them he was to marry the girl who had saved him, and a great feast was made. The maiden became a princess, and she richly deserved all the honours showered upon her.

How Dorothy Became a Princess

An extract from **The Emerald City of Oz**
by L Frank Baum

Dorothy is a little girl from Kansas. She has travelled to the magical land of Oz before, and has now been brought back by Princess Ozma.

WHEN THE PEOPLE of the Emerald City heard that Dorothy had returned to them everyone was eager to see her, for the little girl was a general favourite in the Land of Oz.

She was a simple, sweet and true little girl who was honest to herself and to all whom she met. In this world, simplicity and kindness are the only magic wands that work wonders, and in the Land of Oz, Dorothy found these same qualities had won for her the love and admiration of the people. The little girl had made many friends in the fairy country, and the only real grief the Ozites had ever experienced was when Dorothy left them.

She received a joyful welcome, although no one except Ozma knew at first that she had finally come to stay for good.

Dorothy had four lovely rooms in the palace, which were always reserved for her use and were called 'Dorothy's rooms.' They consisted of a lovely sitting-room, a dressing-room, a dainty bedchamber and a big marble bathroom. In these rooms were everything that her heart could desire, placed there with thoughtfulness by Ozma for her little friend's use.

The royal dressmakers had the little girl's measurements, so they kept the closets in her dressing room filled with lovely dresses of every description and suitable for every occasion. No wonder Dorothy had refrained from bringing her old calico and gingham dresses! Of course Dorothy enjoyed all these luxuries, and the only reason she had preferred to live in Kansas was because her uncle and aunt loved her and needed her with them.

Now, however, all was to be changed, and Dorothy was delighted to know that her dear relatives were to share her good fortune and enjoy the delights of the Land of Oz.

Next morning, at Ozma's request, Dorothy dressed herself in a pretty sky-blue dress of rich silk, trimmed with real pearls. The buckles of her shoes were set with pearls, too, and more of these priceless gems were on a lovely coronet which she wore upon her forehead. "For," said her friend Ozma, "from this time forth, my dear, you must assume your rightful rank as a Princess of Oz, and being my chosen companion you must dress in a way befitting the dignity of your position."

As soon as they had breakfasted in Ozma's pretty boudoir – the Ruler of Oz said, "Now, dear friend, we will transport your uncle and

aunt from Kansas to the Emerald City. But I think it would be fitting, in receiving such distinguished guests, for us to sit in my Throne Room."

So together they went to the Throne Room, an immense domed chamber in the centre of the palace. Here stood the royal throne, made of gold and encrusted with enough precious stones to stock a dozen jewellery stores in our country.

Ozma seated herself in the throne, and Dorothy sat at her feet. In the room were assembled many ladies and gentlemen of the court, clothed in rich apparel and wearing fine jewellery. In a balcony high up in the dome an orchestra played sweet music, and beneath the dome two fountains sent sprays of coloured perfumed water shooting up nearly as high as the arched ceiling.

"Are you ready, Dorothy?" asked Ozma.

"I am," replied Dorothy, "but I don't know whether Aunt Em and Uncle Henry are."

"That won't matter," declared Ozma. "The sooner they begin their new life the happier they will be. Here they come!"

As she spoke, there before the throne appeared Uncle Henry and Aunt Em, who for a moment stood motionless with startled faces. Aunt Em wore a faded, blue-checked apron. Her hair was straggly and she had on a pair of Uncle Henry's old slippers. In one hand she held a dish-towel and in the other a cracked dish, which she had been engaged in wiping when so suddenly transported to the Land of Oz.

Uncle Henry, when the summons came, had been out in the barn 'doin' chores'. He wore a ragged and much soiled straw hat, a checked shirt without any collar and overalls tucked into the tops of his old work boots.

"By gum!" gasped Uncle Henry, looking bewildered.

"Well!" gurgled Aunt Em in a frightened voice. Then her eyes fell upon Dorothy, and she said, "D-d-d-don't that look like our little girl – our Dorothy, Henry?"

But now Dorothy sprang forwards and embraced and kissed her aunt and uncle

affectionately, afterwards taking their hands in her own.

"Don't be afraid," she said to them. "You are now in the Land of Oz, where you are to live always, and be comfer'ble an' happy. You'll never have to worry over anything again, 'cause there won't be anything to worry about. And you owe it all to the kindness of Princess Ozma."

Here she led them before the throne and continued, "Your Highness, this is Uncle Henry and Aunt Em. They want to thank you for bringing them here."

Aunt Em tried to 'slick' her hair, and she hid the dish-towel and dish under her apron while she bowed to the lovely Ozma. Uncle Henry took off his straw hat and held it awkwardly in his hands.

But the Ruler of Oz rose and came from

her throne to greet her newly arrived guests.

"You are very welcome here. I have brought you here for Princess Dorothy's sake," she said, graciously, "and I hope you will be quite happy in your new home." Then she turned to her courtiers, who were silently and gravely regarding the scene, and added, "I present to my people our Princess Dorothy's beloved Uncle Henry and Aunt Em, who will hereafter be subjects of our kingdom. It will please me to have you join me in making them happy and contented."

Hearing this, all those assembled bowed low and respectfully to the old farmer and his wife.

"And now," said Ozma to them, "Dorothy will now show you the rooms I have prepared for you. I hope you will like them, and shall expect you to join me at lunch."

So Dorothy led her relatives away, and as soon as they were out of the Throne Room and alone in the corridor, Aunt Em squeezed Dorothy's hand and said, "Child! How in the world did we ever get here so quick? And is it all real? And are we to stay here, as she says? What does it all mean, anyhow?"

Dorothy laughed.

"Why didn't you tell us what you were goin' to do?" inquired Uncle Henry, reproachfully. "If I'd known about it, I'd 'a put on my Sunday clothes."

"I'll 'splain ever'thing as soon as we get to your rooms," promised Dorothy. "You're in great luck, Uncle Henry and Aunt Em, an' so am I! And oh! I'm so happy to have got you here, at last!"

"An' my hair looks like a fright!" wailed Aunt Em.

"Never mind," returned the little girl, reassuringly. "You won't have anything to do now but to look pretty, Aunt Em, an' Uncle Henry won't have to work until his back aches, that's certain."

"Sure?" they asked, wonderingly, and in the same breath.

"Course I'm sure," said Dorothy. "You're in the Fairyland of Oz, now, an' what's more, you belong to it!"

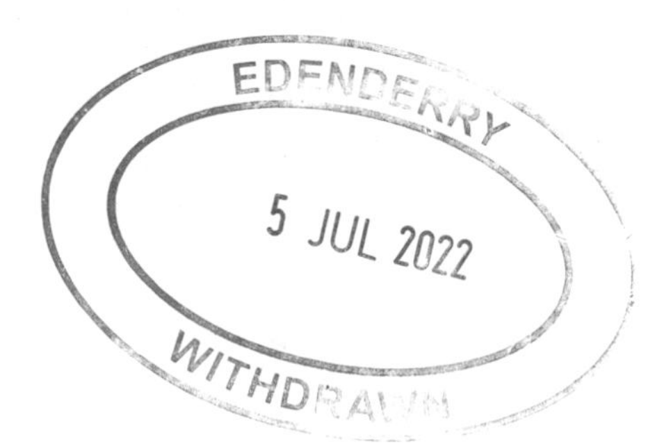